DreamWorks

TrollHunters

Tales of Arcadia

from Guillermo del Toro

DreamWorks

TROLLHUNTERS

TALES OF ARCADIA

FROM GUILLERMO DEL TORO

THE SECRET HISTORY OF TROLLKIND

Script by
MARC GUGGENHEIM &
RICHARD HAMILTON

Art by
TIMOTHY GREEN II

Coloring by
WES DZIOBA

Lettering by
RICHARD STARKINGS
and Comicraft's
JIMMY BETANCOURT

Cover Art by
BILL SIENKIEWICZ

Dark Horse Books

president and publisher
MIKE RICHARDSON

editor
FREDDYE MILLER

collection designer
JUSTIN COUCH

assistant editor
KEVIN BURKHALTER

digital art technician
ALLYSON HALLER

Special thanks to Rodrigo Blaas, A.C. Bradley, Corinne Combs, Marc Guggenheim, Dan Hageman, Kevin Hageman, Lawrence "Shifty" Hamashima, Chad Hammes, Kelly Kulchak, Barbara Layman, Christina Steinberg, Mike Sund, John Tanzer, Andrew Tolbert, Alex Ward, and Susan Weber at DreamWorks Animation and Universal Studios.

Trollhunters: Tales of Arcadia—The Secret History of Trollkind

Published by Dark Horse Books
A division of Dark Horse Comics, Inc.
10956 SE Main Street
Milwaukie, OR 97222

DarkHorse.com

International Licensing: 503-905-2377
To find a comics shop in your area, visit comicshoplocator.com

Names: Guggenheim, Marc, author. | Hamilton, Richard, author. | Green, Timothy, II, 1975- artist. | Dzioba, Wes, colourist. | Comicraft, letterer. | Sienkiewicz, Bill, artist.
Title: Trollhunters : the secret history of trollkind / script by Marc Guggenheim & Richard Hamilton ; art by Timothy Green II ; coloring by Wes Dzioba ; lettering by Comicraft ; cover art by Bill Sienkiewicz.
Description: First edition. | Milwaukie, OR : Dark Horse Books, 2018. | Summary: "When fifteen-year-old teenager Jim Lake, Jr. stumbled upon a magical amulet, it gave him a powerful suit of armor and the title of Trollhunter--defender of the good Trolls. In one training session, Jim's Troll companion, Blinky, must detail the battles of Kanjigar the Courageous--his struggles, triumphs, and failures in leading the safety of Troll Market!"-- Provided by publisher.
Identifiers: LCCN 2017045876 | ISBN 9781506702896 (paperback)
Subjects: LCSH: Graphic novels. | CYAC: Graphic novels. | Trolls--Fiction. | Magic--Fiction. | BISAC: JUVENILE FICTION / Comics & Graphic Novels / Media Tie-In. | JUVENILE FICTION / Comics & Graphic Novels / General.
Classification: LCC PZ7.7.G84 Tr 2018 | DDC 741.5/973--dc23
LC record available at https://lccn.loc.gov/2017045876

First edition: February 2018
ISBN 978-1-50670-289-6

1 3 5 7 9 10 8 6 4 2
Printed in China

Human teenager Jim Lake, Jr. possesses the magical amulet that grants him access to a powerful suit of armor and the monumental responsibility of Trollhunter—defender of the good Trolls. Along with his friends—both human and troll—he trains to fight for the Trolls that live beneath his hometown of Arcadia Oaks.

TROLLMARKET. THE HERO'S FORGE.
THIS COULD BE GOING BETTER.

INDEED.
THOUGH IF THERE WERE NO ROOM FOR IMPROVEMENT, THERE WOULD BE NO NEED FOR TRAINING.

EXCELLENT, MASTER JIM! YOU HAVE HIM RIGHT WHERE YOU WANT HIM!

SERIOUSLY?
IT'S CALLED "POSITIVE REINFORCEMENT."
I READ A BOOK ON IT.
AAARRGGHH!!!, WOULD YOU PLEASE?

IT'S NO USE.
GUNMAR IS GONNA MOP THE FLOOR WITH ME...
DOUBTFUL, MASTER JIM. TROLLS AREN'T KNOWN FOR THEIR CLEANING HABITS.

OH, IT'S AN IDIOM.
YES, I'M AFRAID IF WE CONTINUE ALONG OUR PRESENT COURSE, THE FLOORS OF ARCADIA OAKS WILL BE QUITE CLEAN INDEED.
THANKS FOR THE ENCOURAGEMENT.

I SAID "ALONG OUR PRESENT COURSE."

WHAT'S NEEDED HERE IS AN INSPIRATIONAL RECITATION OF--
DON'T SAY "TROLL HISTORY."
--TROLL LORE.

PLEASE NOT ANOTHER HISTORY LESSON...
AT LEAST IT BEATS GETTING BEATEN UP.
THAT'S SADLY TRUE.

HISTORY IS NEVER SAD, MASTER JIM.
YOU CAN DRAW BOTH SOLACE AND INSPIRATION FROM THE FACT THAT YOU ARE ONLY THE LATEST IN A LONG LINE OF TROLLHUNTERS.
EACH OF WHOM FACED CHALLENGES AS GREAT OR EVEN GREATER THAN THE ONE YOU FACE NOW.

INDEED, EVEN DRAAL'S OWN FATHER--
KANJIGAR THE COURAGEOUS.
--SUFFERED MANY CRISES OF SELF-CONFIDENCE.
SEE, JIMBO? EVEN KANJIGAR.
WHAT TYPES OF CRISES?
WOULD YOU BELIEVE THAT EVEN THE GREAT KANJIGAR DOUBTED HIS FITNESS TO HOLD THE MANTLE OF TROLLHUNTER?

IN FACT, I ***WOULD*** BELIEVE IT.

ALL RIGHT, BLINK. LAY IT ON ME.
LAY IT ON US.
LOVE STORYTIME.
AS DO I.

AND THE BEGINNING OF THIS STORY REQUIRES US TO RETURN TO THE END...

"THE END OF THE THREAT OF THE GUMM-GUMMS.
"I SPEAK, OF COURSE, OF THE GREAT BATTLE OF KILLAHEAD BRIDGE."

"I WAS THERE THAT FATEFUL NIGHT AND FOUGHT QUITE GALLANTLY.
PLEASE DON'T EAT ME!!!
"DRAAL FOUGHT SIDE-BY-SIDE WITH HIS FATHER KANJIGAR, WHO HAD YET TO BE CHOSEN AS THE TROLLHUNTER AMULET'S MASTER.

"THAT MANTLE WAS CARRIED MOST ABLY BY..."

OOO! OOO! I KNOW THAT ONE!
IT'S DEYA THE DELIVERER!
INDEED, TOBY D.
DON'T INTERRUPT ME AGAIN.
BUT DEYA HAD NOT EARNED THE NAME "DELIVERER" BY THIS POINT.

"NOR HAD AAARRRGGHH!!! RENOUNCED THE GUMM-GUMM PATH.
"UNTIL THAT FATEFUL NIGHT."

"WHEN UPON SEEING KANJIGAR AT BULAR'S MERCY...

"...HE HEARD THE CALL OF HIS CONSCIENCE."

FATHER!!!
"IN A CERTAIN FORM.

"AND, IN THAT MOMENT, AAARRRGGHH!!! CHANGED SIDES."

"HE CLASHED WITH THE MIGHTY BULAR...

"...AND DEALT HIM AN EVEN MIGHTIER BLOW."
KACHOK

AND RAN.
INDEED.

"SO GREAT WAS AAARRGGHH!!!'S INNER TURMOIL, HE FLED FROM THE FIELD OF BATTLE, TORN AND CONFLICTED."

"BULAR GAVE CHASE.

"AND THAT IS WHY NEITHER WAS PRESENT FOR...THE CONVERGENCE."

WHAT'S THE CONVERGENCE?
WHAT DID I SAY ABOUT INTERRUPTING?
NOT TO.
PRECISELY.

"THE CONVERGENCE IS WHAT HAS BECOME KNOWN AS THE MOMENT WHEN DEYA MANAGED TO STRIKE A CRITICAL BLOW AGAINST GUNMAR

"AND THEN PLACED HER AMULET WITHIN THE STONE OF KILLAHEAD BRIDGE..."

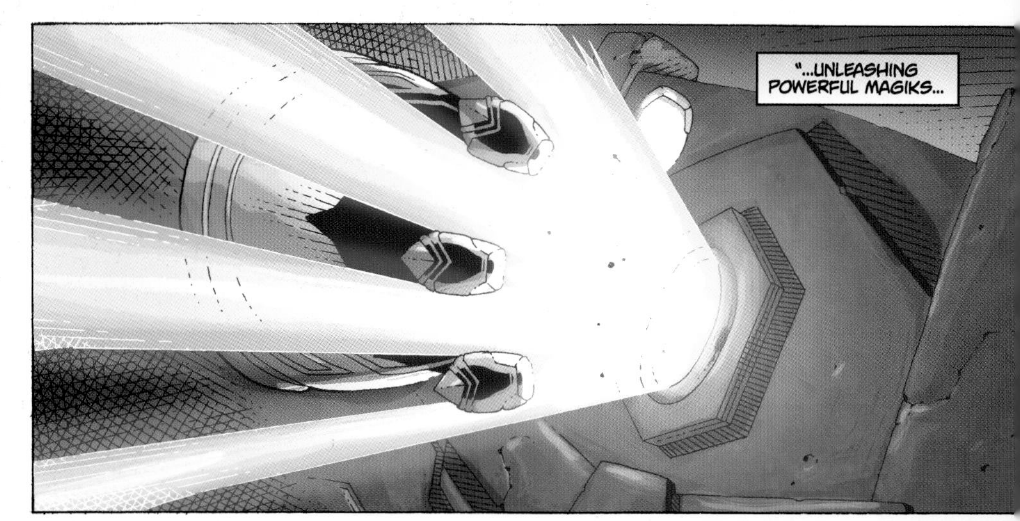
"...UNLEASHING POWERFUL MAGIKS...

"...WHICH BANISHED ALL GUMM-GUMMS PRESENT...

"...TO THE DARKLANDS."

"ALAS, IT WAS A BITTERSWEET VICTORY, AS IT APPEARED MY BROTHER--"
"WAIT. YOU'VE GOT A **BROTHER?**"
RIGHT. NO INTERRUPTING. GOT IT.
"MY BROTHER, DICTATIOUS GALADRIGAL.
"APPARENTLY, HE FELL IN THE COURSE OF BATTLE."

AND I WOULD NEVER SEE HIM AGAIN.
SO PROFOUND WAS MY GRIEF I BARELY HEARD DEYA ORDER US TO DISMANTLE THE KILLAHEAD BRIDGE SO GUNMAR AND HIS HORDE COULD ***NEVER*** ESCAPE FROM THEIR EXILE IN THE DARKLANDS.
DISMANTLE THE KILLAHEAD BRIDGE SO GUNMAR AND HIS HORDE CAN ***NEVER*** ESCAPE FROM THEIR EXILE IN THE DARKLANDS.

"THE PIECES WERE TAKEN BY SEVERAL VOLUNTEER TROLLS AND SCATTERED TO THE FOUR CORNERS OF THE EARTH.
"CENTURIES PASSED--"
"WAITAMINUTE..."

CENTURIES? THE KILLAHEAD BRIDGE IS DISMANTLED AND THE GUMM-GUMMS ARE BANISHED.
ISN'T THE STORY OVER?
IT'S THE STORYTELLER WHO DETERMINES THE TALE'S CONCLUSION, MASTER JIM.

WE HAVEN'T EVEN GOTTEN TO THE PART WHERE KANJIGAR ASSUMES THE MANTLE YOU FEEL UNWORTHY TO BEAR.
WELL, I NEVER SAID--

NO INTERRUPTING. SORRY.

NOW, AS I WAS SAYING...

"CENTURIES PASSED.
"AND A FEEBLE TRUCE--KNOWN AS 'THE PACT'--WAS STRUCK BETWEEN MANKIND AND TROLLKIND.

"BUT AS THE YEARS WENT BY, A CONSERVATIVE SEGMENT OF TROLLS GREW RESTLESS.
"THEY LONGED FOR THE GUMM-GUMMS' BRUTALITY AND STRENGTH. THEY BELIEVED THE PACT MADE US LOOK WEAK. THAT HUMANS 'LOOKED DOWN' UPON US.
"AND AS THIS HAPPENED, THE HEARTSTONE--THE SOURCE OF OUR HOME'S SUSTENANCE AND VITALITY--BEGAN TO WANE."

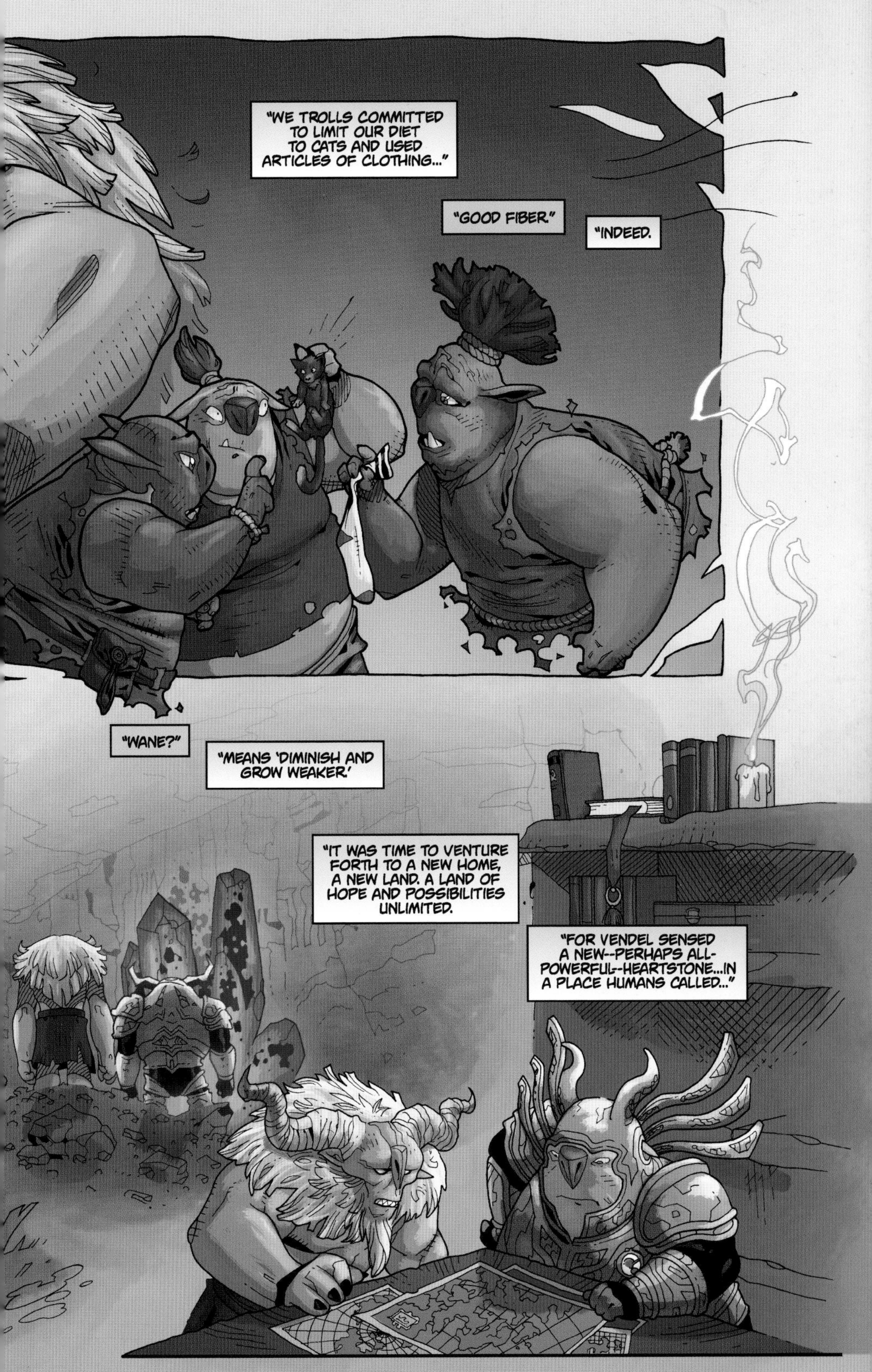
"WE TROLLS COMMITTED TO LIMIT OUR DIET TO CATS AND USED ARTICLES OF CLOTHING..."
"GOOD FIBER."
"INDEED.
"WANE?"
"MEANS 'DIMINISH AND GROW WEAKER.'
"IT WAS TIME TO VENTURE FORTH TO A NEW HOME, A NEW LAND. A LAND OF HOPE AND POSSIBILITIES UNLIMITED.
"FOR VENDEL SENSED A NEW--PERHAPS ALL-POWERFUL--HEARTSTONE...IN A PLACE HUMANS CALLED..."

"...THE NEW WORLD."
THIS FLOATING HUMAN MARKET SETS SAIL AT SUNRISE.

WHICH DOESN'T GIVE US MUCH TIME. TREAD LIGHTLY. AND MAKE HASTE.
WORRY NOT, DEYA.
ALTHOUGH SURFACE VILLAGES LIKE THIS "PLYMOUTH" SEEM UNSETTLING, EVEN LAUGHABLE, TO US--WE TROLLS REMAIN SUPREMELY COMFORTABLE UNDER COVER OF DARKNESS.

THAT'S WHAT WORRIES ME.
FOR I SENSE DANGER.

TROLLHUNTER!

CRE-ACK
THE SCION OF GUNMAR WOULD WASH AWAY OLD GRIEVANCES--
--WITH A RIVER OF YOUR BLOOD!
ALL OF YOU--TO THE MAYFLOWER.

I'LL DEAL WITH BULAR.
CLANG

DEYA! DRAAL THE DEADLY STANDS FAST AT YOUR SIDE--
NO! OUR TROLLHUNTER'S GIVEN US A CHANCE AT SURVIVAL. LET'S NOT SQUANDER IT.
BUT, FATHER, SHE--SHE'S ONE OF US...

"YES, SON. AND WHAT SHE DOES-- SHE DOES FOR ALL OF US."
YOU FOUGHT HARDER AT KILLAHEAD, TROLLHUNTER.
NOT ENOUGH FLESHLING IN YOUR DIET NOW?
THE THOUGHT OF VANQUISHING YOU IS ALL THE NOURISHMENT I NEED, GUMM-GUMM.

STEP THE MAST SMARTLY, LADS!
SHEET HOME AND RAISE ANCHOR!
MAKE READY TO SET SAIL!
THE HUMANS ARE PUNCTUAL, I'LL GIVE THEM THAT.

THAT'S IT, TROLLHUNTER-- RUN!
I'LL HOUND YOU DOWN AS I HAVE ACROSS THIS LAND! ACROSS CENTURIES!
GOOD...

..I HAD HOPED AS MUCH.
THOOM

IT WOULD SEEM NEITHER OF US SHALL SET FOOT ON THE NEW WORLD, BULAR.
A SMALL PRICE TO PAY--

"--FOR THE SAFE PASSAGE OF MY PEOPLE."

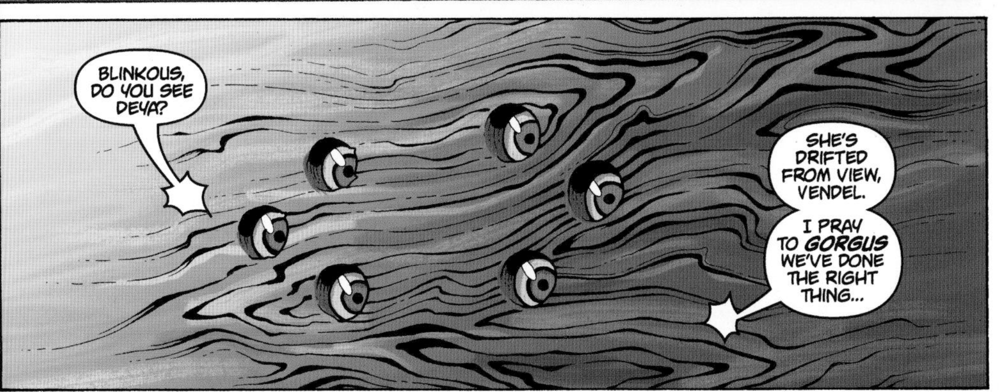
BLINKOUS, DO YOU SEE DEYA?
SHE'S DRIFTED FROM VIEW, VENDEL.
I PRAY TO GORGUS WE'VE DONE THE RIGHT THING...

MAY MERLIN GRANT YOU GREATER MERCY THAN ANY *YOU* HAVE SHOWN, BULAR.
MERCY?
NO. NO MERCY...

BUT I OFFER *BLINDING SUNLIGHT* INSTEAD...

AAAGH!

A PITY YOU CAN'T *WATCH* ME SLAUGHTER YOUR KIND, TROLLHUNTER.

MY EYES MAY NOT SEE--

--BUT THE AMULET STILL GIVES ME SIGHT.
SP-TANG
URK!

REALLY, TROLLHUNTER?

DID YOUR "AMULET" SEE THAT COMING?
SHUNK

AND I WILL TAKE THAT ACCURSED AMULET IN MY FATHER'S NAME...
I WON'T FAIL YOU FATHERRR-

--RRRRRRRRAGH!
SSSZZZSSS

WELL? WHAT'RE YOU--WAITING FOR?

"GO."
FASWOOSH

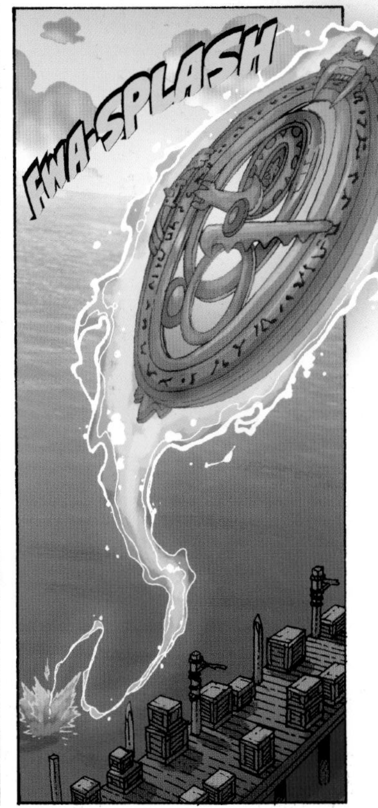
FWA-SPLASH

WHA--? LOOK, MEN! A KELPIE!
'TIS NO KELPIE, YE DAFT JACK-TAR!
TICK
TICK
TICK
TICK
WHATEVER IT IS LOOKS RIGHT FANCY! SNARE IT!
TICK
MROW HSS
NEEP! EEK! NEEP!
NEEP! EEK! NEEP!
REPENT AND CRY WOE, YE SINNERS! 'TIS JUDGEMENT DAY, COME TO CLAIM OUR LOT!
TICK
ARE YOU SURE? IT SEEMS MORE LIKE A FLYING CLOCK.
TICK
DOESN'T MATTER--STILL EVIL! THE DEVIL TAKES MANY FORMS!
NEEP! EEK! NEEP!
THE AMULET! THEN OUR CHAMPION HAS FALLEN...DEYA! MAY THE VOID TAKE YOU AND KEEP YOU!
TICK
TICK
TICK
OH, MY--BUT THIS IS A SURPRISE! THAT SAID, A MOMENT OF SUCH IMPORT DESERVES A FEW WORDS OF STAID COMMEMORATION.
AHEM I, BLINKOUS GALADRIGAL, DO HEREBY HUMBLY, YET VALIANTLY, ACCEPT THE MANTLE OF--

--OH.
TICK TICK TICK

TICK
TICK
TING

FOR THE GLORY OF MERLIN--
--DAYLIGHT IS MINE TO COMMAND!
THOUGH I KNOW NOT WHY...
F-FATHER?

MERLIN BLESSED THE AMULET WITH A SIGHT OF ITS OWN. IT CHOOSES FOR ITSELF.
YOU ABOVE ALL OTHERS UNDERSTAND SACRIFICE, KANJIGAR-- AT KILLAHEAD, ON THIS JOURNEY, MY OWN, AND BEYOND...
I HAVE POINTED OUR PEOPLE TO THE NEW WORLD. TO HOPE.
BUT IF THEY ARE TO REACH IT, WHAT THEY SHALL REQUIRE MOST OF ALL...

...IS COURAGE.
"SUFFICE IT TO SAY, OUR VOYAGE ACROSS THE ATLANTIC WAS FRAUGHT WITH HARDSHIP.
"FOR HUMANS AND TROLLS ALIKE."

AGAIN?! THAT'S TWICE IN ONE WEEK OUR LINES HAVE GONE MISSING!
SURELY YOU DON'T SUSPECT YOUR GOD-FEARING PASSENGERS OF SUCH PERFIDY!
SLRP

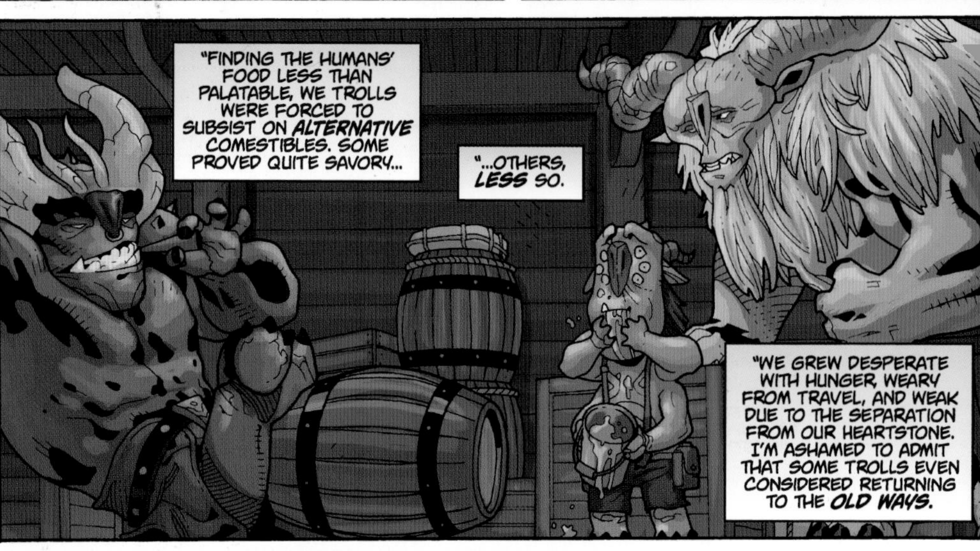
"FINDING THE HUMANS' FOOD LESS THAN PALATABLE, WE TROLLS WERE FORCED TO SUBSIST ON ALTERNATIVE COMESTIBLES. SOME PROVED QUITE SAVORY...
"...OTHERS, LESS SO.
"WE GREW DESPERATE WITH HUNGER, WEARY FROM TRAVEL, AND WEAK DUE TO THE SEPARATION FROM OUR HEARTSTONE. I'M ASHAMED TO ADMIT THAT SOME TROLLS EVEN CONSIDERED RETURNING TO THE OLD WAYS.

"I WON'T NAME NAMES."
FORGET THE PACT! WE'RE STARVING! AND THERE'S AN ENTIRE COLONY OF NUTRITIOUS HUMANS RIGHT ABOVE OUR HEADS!
HMM. BLINKY HAS A POINT. A VERY TASTY POINT...
BUSHIGAL! AS IF IT WASN'T BAD ENOUGH YOU WENT THROUGH ALL THE SHIP'S CATS IN ONE DAY!
IS THIS HOW YOU HONOR DEYA'S MEMORY?

MONTHS PASS...
I'M LOSING THEM, DRAAL. IF OUR PEOPLE WERE EVER MINE TO BEGIN WITH.
DEYA'S DEAD, FATHER. CLINGING TO HER GHOST DOES US NO FAVORS.
LEAST OF ALL YOU.

PERHAPS I MAY BE OF SOME SLIGHT ASSISTANCE, KANJIGAR! THE TROLLHUNTER MUST BE TRAINED AS MUCH IN LEADERSHIP AS IN COMBAT.
WASN'T UNKAR THE UNFORTUNATE THE LAST TO SUFFER YOUR "SLIGHT ASSISTANCE?"

I'LL HAVE YOU KNOW WE CALLED HIM UNKAR THE ULTIMATE DURING HIS TIME AS TROLLHUNTER!
ALL SIX HOURS OF IT...

DRAAL. BLINKY. BEHOLD!

LAND, HO!
"BY DEYA'S GRACE, WE HAD FINALLY REACHED OUR DESTINATION--AND HELD UP OUR END OF THE PACT, DESPITE CONSIDERABLE TEMPTATION.
GREAT GRONKA MORKA!
"PLYMOUTH ROCK, THE HUMANS CALLED THEIR NEW HOME. IT WAS NO HEARTSTONE, TO BE SURE.
"YET THE VERY SIGHT OF IT RAISED OUR SPIRITS AND GRANTED US THE VIGOR TO EMBARK UPON THE NEXT LEG OF OUR TREK..."

"...TO A PLACE
CALLED 'NEW JERSEY.'

"WE KEPT MOVING.

"YEARS PASSED.
"OUR JOURNEY WAS
TREACHEROUS."

"BUT WE SAW THE WIDE VARIETY OF HUMAN CULTURES THIS 'NEW WORLD' HAD TO OFFER.

"SOME WERE EVEN *USEFUL*.

"AS WERE SOME HUMANS.
"TWO GENTLEMEN NAMED 'LEWIS' AND 'CLARK' WERE PARTICULARLY HELPFUL IN GUIDING US ON OUR PATH."

"BUT NEITHER LEWIS NOR CLARK COULD AID US IN OUR MOST FORMIDABLE CHALLENGE. DUE TO THE PROLONGED SEPARATION FROM A HEARTSTONE, OUR BODIES GREW WEAKER.
"WE WERE FORCED TO STOP AND SLUMBER IN CAVES BETWEEN OUR MARCHES--OFTEN FOR MONTHS AT A TIME. THESE HIBERNATIONS DELAYED OUR WESTWARD PROGRESS GREATLY. AND WITH DELAY COMES...FRUSTRATION."
DARN!
SPAK
I SEE YOU'VE TAKEN TO ADOPTING HUMAN TURNS OF PHRASE?
THEY DO HAVE A WAY WITH WORDS.
FILTHY CREATURES. ALTHOUGH YOUR PROTECTION OF THEM THROUGH ADHERENCE TO THE PACT IS COMMENDABLE.
AS IS YOUR FORTITUDE. DENYING OUR PEOPLE--YOURSELF, EVEN--FROM SUCH TASTY SUSTENANCE? ON PRINCIPLE?
I MEAN--WHAT IS A "PRINCIPLE" ANYWAY? IT FEELS LIKE A HUMAN CONSTRUCTION.
I SUPPOSE THAT DEPENDS, SEER. DO YOU ASK FOR OUR PEOPLE--
--OR FOR YOURSELF?

DEVILS!

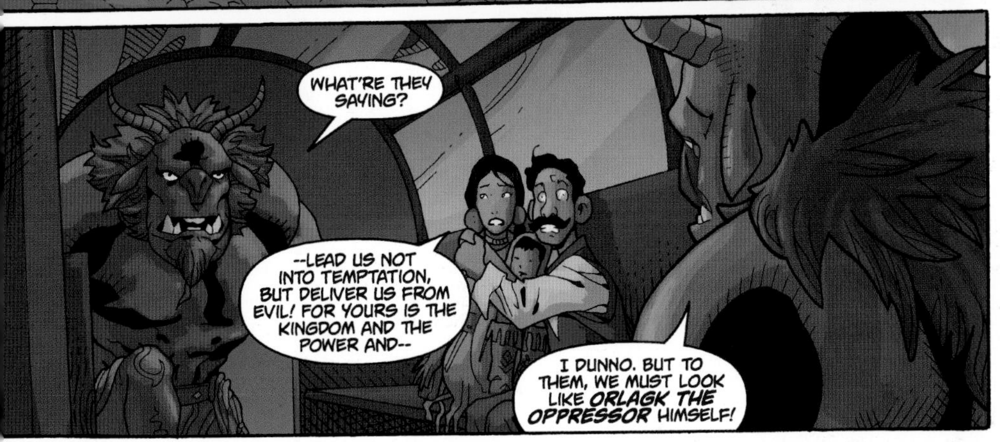
WHAT'RE THEY SAYING?
--LEAD US NOT INTO TEMPTATION, BUT DELIVER US FROM EVIL! FOR YOURS IS THE KINGDOM AND THE POWER AND--
I DUNNO. BUT TO THEM, WE MUST LOOK LIKE ORLAGK THE OPPRESSOR HIMSELF!

--THE GLORY?

"AMEN."
THINK ≶HUFF≶ WE LOST HIM!
WITH ALL THAT ARMOR ≶HUFF≶ NO WAY ≶HUFF≶ KANJIGAR CAN CATCH--

--UHHHFFF!
WHUP
WHUP

MASTERFULLY DONE, KANJIGAR! I WITNESSED YOUR ENTIRE HUNT FROM AFAR AND, WELL--SHEER PERFECTION.
THAT SAID, I DO HAVE A FEW NOTES...

I'LL TAKE THEM UNDER ADVISEMENT. LATER
OF COURSE. AND HAVE YOU CONSIDERED--
LATER.
NATURALLY. BUT IF I COULD JUST OFFER--
LATER.

THIS IS A FINE SETTLEMENT YOU'VE FOUND FOR OUR PEOPLE, FATHER...
THAT IT IS, DRAAL.
IT'S UNFORTUNATE WE MUST ABANDON IT.

ABANDON? BUT--WHY?
FOR THE SAME REASON THE ORIGINAL INHABITANTS LEFT--HUMANS.
ONE TRIBE OVERTOOK ANOTHER, JUST AS THEY'LL DO TO US WHEN WE'RE FOUND.

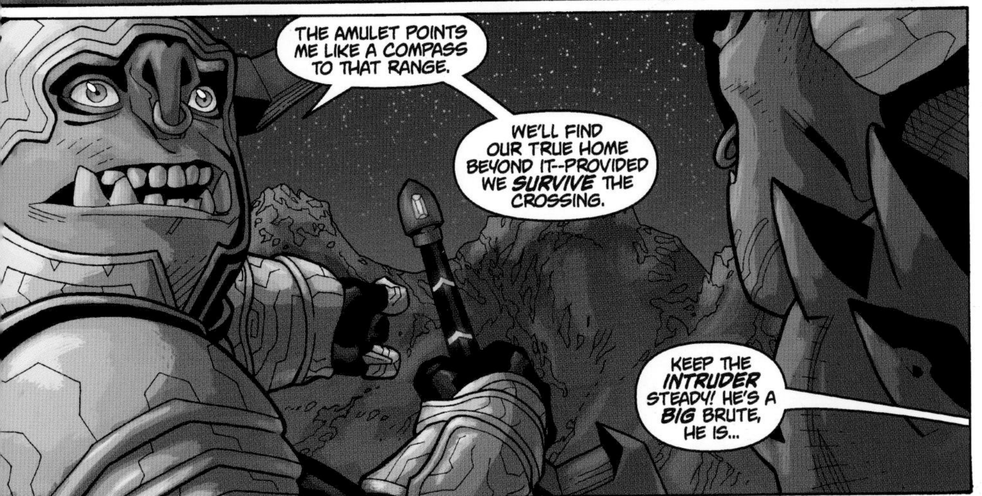
THE AMULET POINTS ME LIKE A COMPASS TO THAT RANGE.
WE'LL FIND OUR TRUE HOME BEYOND IT--PROVIDED WE SURVIVE THE CROSSING.
KEEP THE INTRUDER STEADY! HE'S A BIG BRUTE, HE IS...

...KRUBERA FILTH.
HOLD. WHAT GOES ON HERE?

WE FOUND THIS ONE HIDING IN A GEYSER OPENING BEYOND THAT RIDGE--
--NO DOUBT LYING IN WAIT TO ATTACK US!

I...RECOGNIZE YOU. YOU'VE COME A LONG WAY FROM KILLAHEAD, FRIEND.
BUT HOW?
MISSED BOAT...

"...BY A LITTLE.
"COULDN'T FIND ANOTHER SHIP.
"SAILORS ALL YELL *'AIEEE!'* WHEN SEE ME.

"SO WALKED."
"WALKED? *ALL* THIS TIME? ALL THIS *WAY?*"
"DEEP CAVE TROLLS PATIENT. AND GOOD WITH DIRECTIONS.

"MADE A *FEW* WRONG TURNS..."

...BUT FINALLY FOUND YOU.
A MISTAKE YOU'LL NOT LIKELY REPEAT, STRANGER.
I SAY WE *EXECUTE* HIM!

HE MAY HAVE FOUGHT AT KILLAHEAD, BUT CERTAINLY NOT ON *OUR* SIDE.
FOR ALL WE KNOW, HE MIGHT BE AN ADVANCE SCOUT FOR A *LARGER* FORCE OF ENEMY TROLLS!

WHY, I'D HAZARD THAT THE BUNDLE ON HIS BACK IS SOME SORT OF *WEAPON* TO BE USED AGAINST US!
NOT WEAPON.

GIFT.

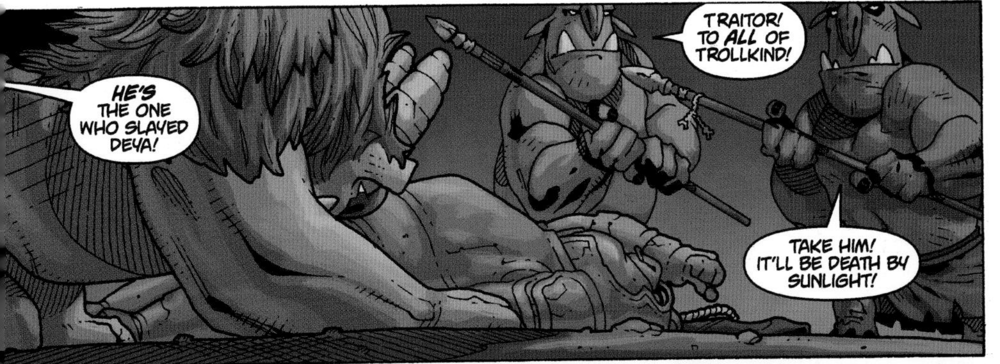
HE'S THE ONE WHO SLAYED DEYA!
TRAITOR! TO ALL OF TROLLKIND!
TAKE HIM! IT'LL BE DEATH BY SUNLIGHT!

THEN I, TOO, SHALL PERISH AT DAYBREAK.
I CARE NOT WHAT YOU THINK. THIS TROLL ONCE RISKED HIS LIFE TO SAVE MY OWN.

I REPAY THAT KINDNESS NOW--AND EXPECT EACH OF YOU TO DO THE SAME.

VENDEL, YOU SIMPLY CANNOT ALLOW--
CONSIDER YOUR PROTESTATIONS DULY NOTED, BLINKOUS.
BUT OUR TROLLHUNTER'S WORD IS LAW. THE KRUBERA MAY STAY--
--ALBEIT AS AN OUTCAST ON THE VERY FRINGES OF OUR GROUP.

MAKES NO SENSE, LEAVING BEHIND A PERFECTLY GOOD BURROW...
I'M SURPRISED THE TROLLHUNTER'S AMULET DOESN'T GLOW YELLOW, THE COWARD...

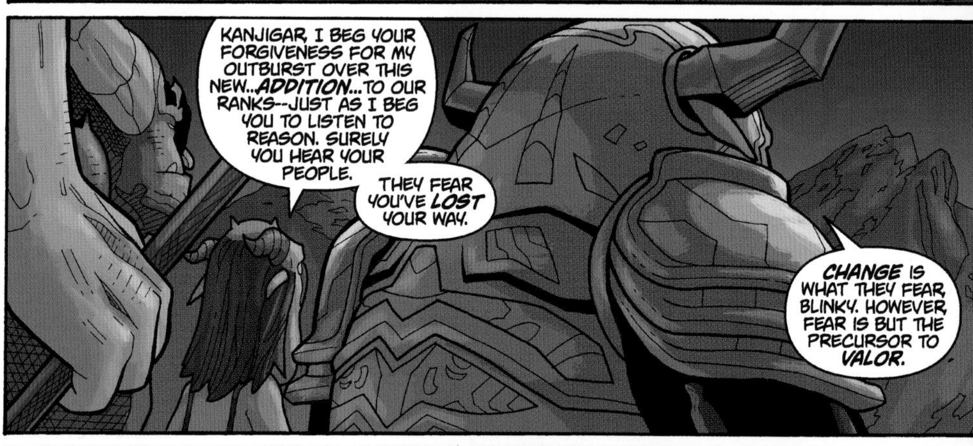
KANJIGAR, I BEG YOUR FORGIVENESS FOR MY OUTBURST OVER THIS NEW...ADDITION...TO OUR RANKS--JUST AS I BEG YOU TO LISTEN TO REASON. SURELY YOU HEAR YOUR PEOPLE.
THEY FEAR YOU'VE LOST YOUR WAY.
CHANGE IS WHAT THEY FEAR, BLINKY. HOWEVER, FEAR IS BUT THE PRECURSOR TO VALOR.

THE DEEDS OF MY FRIEND, AARGHAUMONT, HAVE TAUGHT ME THAT.
YES, YES, THAT'S VERY MOVING, BUT--
"IF KANJIGAR HEEDED MY WARNING THAT DAY, HE DIDN'T SHOW IT.
"AND TO BE HONEST, I SHOULD'VE SAVED MY BREATH..."

"...FOR THE CLIMB TO COME."
CRRRMMMMBBBLLL

AVALANCHE!

KRRRAAASSSHHH
KANJIGAR!

SAVE USSssssss
QUICK! DIG OUT THE OTHERS!

EASY, WISE ONE. I HAVE GOT YOU.
I'LL THANK YOU TO KINDLY KEEP YOUR TRAITOROUS HANDS TO YOURSELF!
"FROZEN FROM OUR HOOVES TO OUR HORNS AND DEPRIVED OF A HEARTSTONE'S RECUPERATIVE PROPERTIES, THE ORDEAL BROUGHT OUT THE WORST IN SOME OF US..."

THOUGHT I FELT AN ITCH.

TELL CRAGGEN-- WHAT MAKES YOU FOOLISH ENOUGH TO BELIEVE HE'D LET YOU SCALE HIS GLORIOUS FORM WITHOUT PAYMENT?
WE HAVE NO QUARREL WITH YOU, OLD ONE.
MERELY DO AS YOUR TROLLHUNTER COMMANDS AND LET US PASS.

AH, NOW, NOW, KANJIGAR! NO NEED TO ANTAGONIZE A FELLOW TROLL!
ESPECIALLY ONE SO LARGE. LET ME HANDLE THIS DIPLOMATICALLY.
GREETINGS, CRAGGEN! I AM VENDEL, SON OF RUNDLE, SON OF KILFRED!
THOUGH THE MOUNTAIN TROLLS HAVE LONG SIDED WITH THE GUMM-GUMMS, I IMPLORE--

OH, I HAVE NO PROBLEM WITH YOU.
IT'S MY BROTHERS WHO HATE MERLIN-WORSHIPPERS.
KILFRED, EH? WE HEARD OF 'IM.
AND THAT HE WAS A REAL GLORK-HOLE.

AH. WELL. I TRIED...
A MOST HEROIC EFFORT, VENDEL. TRULY.

HURR, HURR, HURR! DO NOT POUT, INSIGNIFICANT THINGS--REJOICE!
THERE'S NO NEED TO PASS. YOU'VE REACHED YOUR NEW HOME AT LONG LAST!
HERE, YOU WILL GLADLY SERVE US FOR WHAT REMAINS OF YOUR FLEETING LIVES.
CONSIDER THAT YOUR PAYMENT FOR DARING TO CROSS CRAGGEN, GREATEST OF MOUNTAIN TROLLS, AND HIS BROTHERS THREE.

YOU MAY CAMP AT MY FEET AND REST FOR THE DAY. COME THE NEW MOON, MY BROTHERS AND I SHALL PUT YOU TO TASK.

AFTER COMING ALL THIS WAY, THIS IS OUR FATE?

TO TOIL INSIDE FOUR MOUNTAIN TROLLS UNTIL WE CRUMBLE TO DUST?
I COULD REALLY GO FOR A CAT RIGHT NOW!
ALAS, WHAT CHOICE HAVE WE? WE'VE BEEN APART FROM A HEARTSTONE FOR TOO LONG TO PUT UP MUCH OF A FIGHT. PERHAPS...
PERHAPS THIS WAS ALWAYS MEANT TO BE OUR DESTINY.
DESTINY?!

DESTINY IS A GIFT. DEYA GAVE ALL SHE HAD SO THAT WE MIGHT CONTINUE.
I WILL NOT SEE HER SACRIFICE GO TO WASTE.

KANJIGAR, YOU ARE THE FINEST WARRIOR MY EYES HAVE EVER BEHELD--EVEN IF YOU NEVER DID LET ME TRAIN YOU. BUT TO THINK YOU ALONE CAN TAKE ON A FAMILY OF INBRED MOUNTAIN TROLLS?
IT'S MADNESS!
THE ONLY MADNESS WOULD BE FOR ME TO GIVE UP AND FAIL YOU, BLINKY--AND THE REST OF OUR KIND. I DON'T HAVE THAT KIND OF LUXURY, AS YOUR TROLLHUNTER.
OR YOUR FRIEND.
AND HE WON'T BE ALONE.

THIS TIME, I STAND FAST AT MY TROLLHUNTER'S SIDE.
WHAT HE SAID.
SKRINK
KRAK

THE SUN HAS SET. WE THREE SHALL DO OUR BEST TO DISTRACT CRAGGEN AND HIS CLAN.
WHEN THE EARTH SHAKES, THAT'S YOUR SIGNAL TO ESCAPE.
FAREWELL, MY BROTHERS.

GO WITH GORGUS, TROLLHUNTER.
THOUGH I FEAR WE SHALL ALL SOON JOIN YOU IN THE VOID...

IF YOU SHOULD FALL, I WILL TAKE UP YOUR ARMOR AND AVENGE YOU.
SON, I PRAY YOU NEVER NEED KNOW THE BURDEN THIS AMULET BRINGS.

AH, SEE HOW THEY COME. BUT WHERE ARE THE REST? YOUR YOUNG? YOUR OLD?
EVEN THEY CAN LOOSEN THE BOULDERS IN OUR BOWELS-- HAH!

YOU HUMBLE US WITH YOUR MOST TEMPTING OFFER. BUT I FEAR WE'D MAKE TERRIBLE SLAVES.
I, MYSELF, AM QUITE CLUMSY...

SEE?
KA-SHUNK

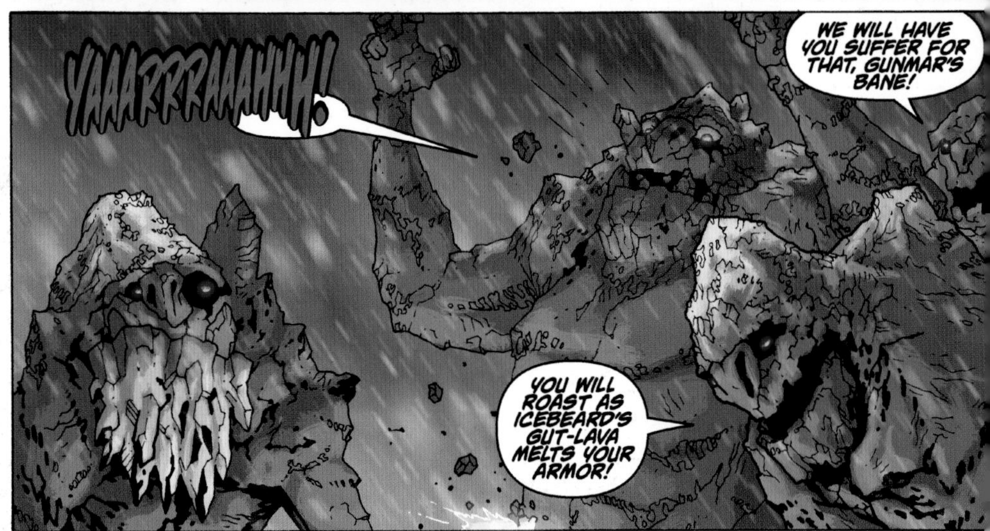
YAAARRRAAAHHH!
WE WILL HAVE YOU SUFFER FOR THAT, GUNMAR'S BANE!
YOU WILL ROAST AS ICEBEARD'S GUT-LAVA MELTS YOUR ARMOR!

RRRMMMMBBBLLLLL
BY UNKAR'S EMPTY BLADDER!
WHY'D WE EVER LEAVE THE OLD COUNTRY? OR AGREE TO THAT BLASTED PACT?!

WHY?
THUMP

MAYBE FOR THE SAME REASON THOSE THREE TROLLS NOW MARCH INTO CERTAIN DEATH!
YOU MEAN THE GUMM-GUMM, DRAAL THE DIM, AND MERLIN'S MISTAKE?
THE ONE WHO WON'T EVEN LET US EAT HUMANS TO RENEW OUR STRENGTH?

I MEAN OUR BROTHERS. I UNDERSTAND YOU'RE AFRAID-- I AM, TOO!
BUT...BUT NEVER FORGET THAT FEAR IS BUT THE PRECURSOR TO VALOR.
THAT TO STRIVE AND TRIUMPH IN THE FACE OF FEAR IS WHAT IT MEANS TO BE A HERO.

TO THINK, I'VE BEEN TRYING TO TRAIN OUR TROLLHUNTER--
--WHEN IT WAS HE WHO TAUGHT ME A LESSON. ONE I HOPE I HAVEN'T LEARNED TOO LATE...

RRRAAAHHH!
KWA-THOOM

ATTACK ONE MOUNTAIN TROLL AND YOU ATTACK US ALL! SO SWEARS BOULDERJAW!
URRK..
THE TIME FOR DISTRACTION IS OVER. THIS IS WAR.
THERE'S STILL FIGHT LEFT IN ME, FATHER.

..BLLLAAAARRRGGG!
MERLIN PRESERVE US...
AARGHAUMONT, ARE YOU READY?

READY.

RRRAAAHHH!!!
FOR THE GLORY OF MERLIN-- ONWARD!
HA-HA-HA-HA-HA!

BWAMM
HNF!

NOT GOOD.

HUH?

YYYAAAAAHHHHH!
KRA-SNAPDD

BLINKY! I'M THANKFUL YOU'VE JOINED US--BUT TO WHAT END?
IS IT THE OTHERS? ARE THEY IN *DANGER?*
OH, THEY LIVE, KANJIGAR.
THOUGH I SCARCELY KNOW HOW THEY'LL BE ABLE TO *LIVE WITH* THEMSELVES.
I OWE YOU A GREAT APOLOGY.
ALL OF YOU.
SOMETIMES, EVEN HAVING *SIX* EYES PREVENTS ONE FROM SEEING THE *TRUTH.*

I KNOW I'M NOT MUCH OF A WARRIOR! BUT IF I'M DYING TODAY--

WHA-- ?
--THEN THESE FOUR ARMS ARE GOING DOWN *SWINGING!*

NOW, AAARRRGGHH!!!
RRRRR--
--RAAAAHHHH!
KA-KOOOOOM
SLOPEBROW!
BY GORGUS... I THINK OUR ODDS JUST WENT FROM SUICIDAL TO IMPOSSIBLE!
I LIKE THOSE ODDS.

AS DO WE.
YOU HONOR ME--AND DEYA'S MEMORY--WITH YOUR COURAGE, GOOD TROLLS.

NOW, STEEL YOURSELVES FOR BATTLE.
CHAK KA-CHAK

AND WHEN IN DOUBT...
WHISH WHISH

AAAIII-YYYEEEEE!
...ALWAYS KICK THEM IN THE GRONK-NUKS!
KRIK
ACK
KRIK

"IN TIME, OUR KIND CAME TO KNOW THIS BLOODY EVENT AS THE GREAT ROCKY MOUNTAIN TROLL WAR.
"OR G.R.M.T.W., FOR SHORT."

"ALTHOUGH WE LOST MANY TROLLS THAT DAY--SOME FRIENDS, SOME NOT, BUT ALL REMEMBERED--
"--IT WAS THE BIRTH OF A LEGEND. BUT TO KANJIGAR...

"...IT WAS DUTY."
I...ASK YOU... CRAGGEN...AS THE LAST OF YOUR KIN...DO YOU YIELD?

AYE, TROLLHUNTER... WE YIELD.

KAN-JI-GAR! KAN-JI-GAR! KAN-JI-GAR!

GLUG!
HIC
GLUG FOR ALL!

YOU NEEDN'T SIT AT THE FRINGES ANY LONGER, AARGHAUMONT.

ONCE AGAIN, YOU'VE PROVEN YOURSELF IN BATTLE.
THANKS. BUT BATTLE WAS *LAST* FOR ME.
NO MORE. AAARRRGGHH!!! NOW PACIFIC.
HAH! I BELIEVE YOU MEAN TO SAY *"PACIFIST,"* MY FRIEND.
SURE.

"MONTHS PASSED. AND WE ARRIVED IN A REALM KNOWN AS...'CALIFORNIA.'"
WELL? FATHER?

WE... WE HAVE *ARRIVED*.

SKRIK
CRACK ACK

FWASH

YES...WITH THE PROPER CARE AND CULTIVATION--A CUT HERE, A CLEAVE THERE...
...I BELIEVE THIS HEARTSTONE WILL GROW INTO THE FINEST OF THIS OR *ANY* LAND.

"VENDEL FELT IT IN HIS HORNS, JUST AS WE FELT THE YOUNG HEARTSTONE START TO RESTORE OUR ENERGY...
"...THIS WAS *HOME*."

"DEYA MAY HAVE DELIVERED US TO THIS STRANGE CONTINENT...
"...BUT IT WAS KANJIGAR WHO ENCOURAGED US TO SURVIVE IT."
CAN THIS BE? EVEN IN VICTORY, DOES SOMETHING STILL TROUBLE OUR TROLLHUNTER?
NO, BLINKY, THOUGH I FEAR I MUST TROUBLE YOU.
I SEEK TO PAY TRIBUTE HERE TO DEYA--TO ALL OUR FALLEN TROLLHUNTERS--YET I REMAIN UNCERTAIN HOW.
ANY ADVICE?
WHY, KANJIGAR...
THAT IS TO SAY, MASTER KANJIGAR..I BELIEVE I HAVE JUST THE IDEA!
"SO NOW YOU SEE, MASTER JIM. WHEN THE STATUES OF YOUR PREDECESSORS LOOK DOWN UPON YOU IN THE HERO'S FORGE, IT IS NOT WITH DISAPPOINTMENT.
"IT IS WITH UNDERSTANDING. EACH OF MERLIN'S CREATIONS HAVE FACED THEIR OWN UNIQUE CHALLENGES IN THEIR OWN UNIQUE WAYS.
"JUST AS YOU SHALL CONTINUE TO DO."

"FOR A TROLLHUNTER IS SO MUCH MORE THAN A WARRIOR."
FINALLY.
RANCHO ARCADIA
EST. 1875 POP. 86 85 84

"TO BECOME A TROLLHUNTER IS TO BECOME PART OF A CONTINUANCE. A TRADITION."
THEY'RE HERE. I SMELL THE AMULET'S STENCH IN THE AIR.
AND HERE ALL I COULD SMELL WAS THE MANURE.
"A LEGACY THAT ENDURES IN THE SAME WAY ITS CHAMPIONS ENDURE."

THAT'S NOT ALL THAT STINKS HERE, IMPURE.
I RECKON I DON'T KNOW WHAT YOU MEAN, STRANGER.
I'M BUT A HUMBLE TEACHER AT THE LOCAL SCHOOLHOUSE.

ALBEIT ONE WITH A MESSAGE FROM YOUR FATHER...
"FOR ALL TIME."
END.